WARNING!

Scaredy Squirrel insists you check your zippers before reading this book.

For a few happy campers: Thomas, Louis, Geneviève and Phil.

Text and illustrations © 2013 Mélanie Watt

Kids Can Press acknowledges the financial support of the Government of Ontario, through the Ontario Media Development Corporation's Ontario Book Initiative; the Ontario Arts Council; the Canada Council for the Arts; and the Government of Canada, through the CBF, for our publishing activity.

Published in Canada by
Kids Can Press Ltd.
25 Dockside Drive
Toronto, ON M5A 0B5

Published in the U.S. by
Kids Can Press Ltd.
2250 Military Road
Tonawanda, NY 14150

www.kidscanpress.com

The artwork in this book was rendered digitally in Photoshop.
The text is set in Potato Cut.

This book is smyth sewn casebound.
Manufactured in Tseung Kwan O, NT Hong Kong, China, in 4/2013 by Paramount Printing Co. Ltd.

CM 13 0 9 8 7 6 5 4 3 2

LIBRARY AND ARCHIVES CANADA CATALOGUING IN PUBLICATION

Watt, Mélanie, 1975-
     Scaredy Squirrel goes camping / written and illustrated by Mélanie Watt.
ISBN 978-1-894786-86-7
I. Title.
PS8645.A88452829 2013   jC813>.6   C2012-908052-7

Kids Can Press is a ʃorus™ Entertainment company

Mélanie Watt

Scaredy Squirrel

goes camping

KIDS CAN PRESS

MÉLANIE WATT PRODUCTIONS

Scaredy Squirrel never goes camping.
He'd rather be comfortable inside than risk going
out in the rugged wilderness.
Besides, setting up camp seems like a lot of trouble.

A few troublemakers Scaredy Squirrel is afraid could get too close for comfort:

skunks

mosquitoes

quicksand

The Three Bears

penguins

zippers

So he finds a simple way to sit back and enjoy camping from a safe distance.

Scaredy Squirrel sets up his
new television.
But he realizes there's a problem.
He needs to plug it in.

Reaching the nearest electrical
outlet will require major
survival skills.

A few survival supplies Scaredy Squirrel needs to pack:

really long extension cord	popsicles	tomato juice	bag of cement

dictionary	pliers	instant oatmeal	fan

THE WILDERNESS OUTFIT

Netted hat
To dodge bugs

Penny
To bring good luck

Nose plug
To bypass nasty odors

Neckerchief
To scout

Water wings
To stay afloat

Walkie-talkie
To stay in contact

Badge
To signal peaceful intentions

Camouflage jacket
To blend into the great outdoors

Rubber boots
To be quick and dry

THE SCAREDY MOTTO: A prepared camper is a happy camper!

0530 HOURS:
Leave comfort zone.

0531 HOURS:
Run through woods.
Keep a low profile.

0541 HOURS:
Enter campground.

0545 HOURS:
Locate electrical outlet.

0548 HOURS:
Plug in extension cord.

0549 HOURS:
Run back to home base.

0559 HOURS:
Get comfy.
Watch *The Joy of Camping.*

SYMBOLS

Tent area

Play area

RV area

Washrooms

Trash area

Electrical outlet

The comfort zone.

Place a walkie-talkie at foot of tree to stay in contact.

Mosquitoes are itching to get you! Fan yourself to blow off these thirsty critters!

Keep a nose out for skunks. If sprayed, overreact! Wash off the stink with gallons of tomato juice.

THE CAMPGROUND MISSION

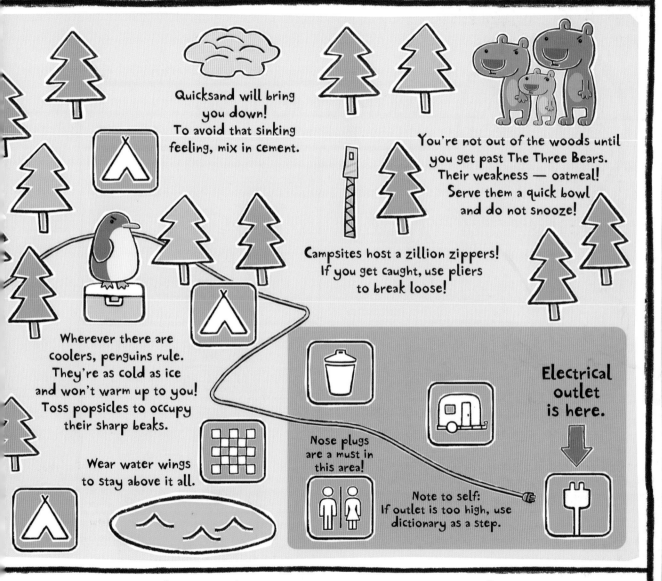

Quicksand will bring you down! To avoid that sinking feeling, mix in cement.

You're not out of the woods until you get past The Three Bears. Their weakness — oatmeal! Serve them a quick bowl and do not snooze!

Campsites host a zillion zippers! If you get caught, use pliers to break loose!

Wherever there are coolers, penguins rule. They're as cold as ice and won't warm up to you! Toss popsicles to occupy their sharp beaks.

Wear water wings to stay above it all.

Electrical outlet is here.

Nose plugs are a must in this area!

Note to self: If outlet is too high, use dictionary as a step.

THE SCAREDY PLEDGE: Planning is everything!

THE RUBBER BOOT CAMP

WARM-UP ROUTINE:
(Repeat 143 times)

1.

2.

3.

4.

THE SCAREDY PROMISE: A fit squirrel is a safe squirrel!

AND FITNESS TRAINING CHARTS

OBSTACLE COURSE PRACTICE RUN:

THE OUTDOOR CONDITIONS

	GO	WAIT	CANCEL
SUN	X		
CLOUD		X	
RAIN		X	
WIND		X	
SNOW		X	
VOLCANO ACTIVITY			X

THE SCAREDY RULE: If all else fails, take cover and play dead!

The following afternoon, right on schedule, Scaredy Squirrel proceeds toward the campground.

Scaredy tugs.

He pulls.

He loop-

the-loops.

But suddenly . . .

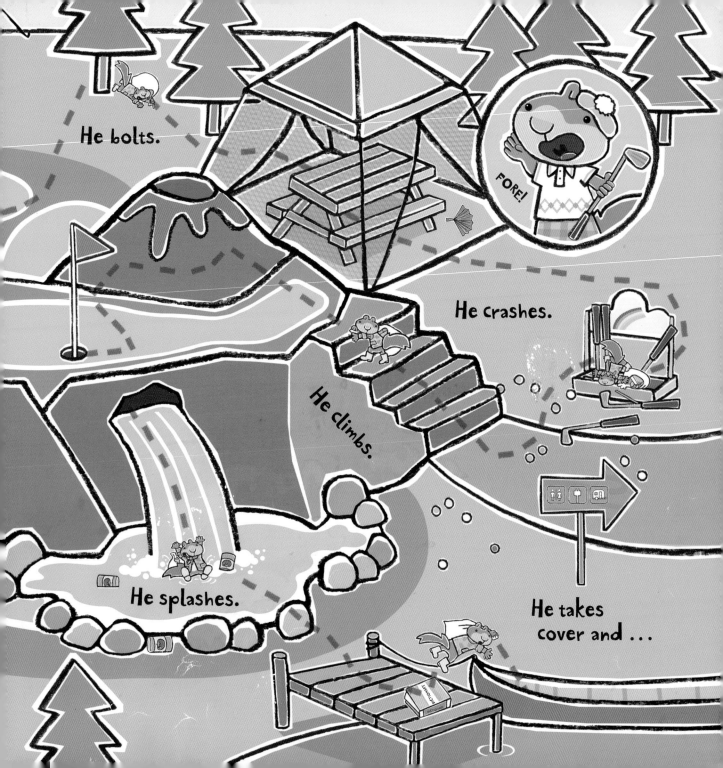

He bolts.

FORE!

He crashes.

He climbs.

He splashes.

He takes
cover and . . .

Scaredy Squirrel finally gets the drift.
He forgets all about the skunks, mosquitoes,
quicksand, Three Bears, penguins and zippers.

The wilderness isn't meant to be seen
from afar, it's meant to be enjoyed
up close!

Scaredy breathes
the fresh air ...

savors roasted
marshmallows ...

gazes up
at the stars ...

gathers
pinecones ...

listens to songs ...

and gets comfortable.

Early the next morning, Scaredy Squirrel plugs in his extension cord and follows it back home.

This wild adventure has inspired him to approach camping differently.

toaster

P.S. Some things are
worth the trouble.